Winter Sports

Jill McDougall

Contents

What Are Winter Sports?

Sports that are played on ice or snow are often called winter sports.

In cold parts of the world, children and their families enjoy many kinds of winter sports.

Some of these are skiing, ice skating, sledding, snow tubing and snowboarding.

Some winter sports are played in teams. Ice hockey and sled hockey are team sports that are played on ice.

Skiing

Children learn to ski
in places that have ice and snow.

A skier wears a pair of skis that are put onto their boots.
Skis are long, flat **runners**
made of metal, plastic or wood.

People can ski with their friends.

Skiers are able to glide across snow or race downhill on skis.

Some skiers carry two light poles that they use to keep their **balance** and make turns.

Think and Talk About ...

Long ago, people used skis when walking from place to place in snow. Now, skis are mainly used in sport.

Ice Skating

Lots of children enjoy ice skating.
People skate at **ice rinks** or on frozen lakes.

Ice skaters wear ice skates.
These are boots or shoes
that have metal blades on the soles.

Think and Talk About ...

A long time ago, ice skaters wore boots with wooden blades.

Ice skaters can move quickly across the ice.

The blades melt the ice as they move along. This gives the skater a smooth ride.

Some skaters can jump and spin through the air. This takes a lot of practice!

Children enjoy doing ice-skating tricks.

Sledding

Many children love to go sledding down a snowy slope.

It is fun to ride a sled with a friend.

People hold on tightly to ropes attached to the runners on a sled.

Some sleds have thin, metal runners to help the sled glide over rough snow.

Sleds can travel very quickly, and people need to take care not to crash.

Snow Tubing

Snow tubing is a sport
the whole family can enjoy together.

People sit inside a tube
and slide down an icy hill.

Snow tubes travel quickly
because they are light.
This gives people an exciting ride.

Think and Talk About ...

Tubes come in many sizes. Sometimes, two or more people can fit inside one tube.

A family rides in their snow tubes.

Snowboarding

Snowboarding is another exciting winter sport.

Riders slide downhill while standing on a snowboard. A snowboard is a flat board with straps to hold the rider's feet in place.

Some children learn to do tricks on their snowboard, such as riding over jumps.

A snowboarder balances carefully on his board.

A long **channel** made of snow can also be used for snowboard tricks. The channel is called a half-pipe. Riders **leap** above the edge of the half-pipe to do amazing twists and turns in the air.

Snowboarders must wear proper safety gear when riding on a half-pipe.

Think and Talk About ...

Snowboarding is a sport at the Winter Olympics.

Ice Hockey

Ice hockey is a sport played by two teams. The game is played on an ice rink, and the players wear ice skates.

There is a goal net at each end of the rink.

Hockey players wear masks to protect their faces.

Each team has 20 players,
but only six are on the rink at one time.
The players use hockey sticks
to send the **puck** into their goal net.

The goalkeeper tries to stop
the other team from scoring goals.

Think and Talk About ...

Ice-hockey pucks are frozen, so they do not bounce during the games.

Sled Hockey

Sled hockey is a game for people who cannot skate standing up.

Sled hockey is like ice hockey, but the players move around on a sled.

The hockey sticks have spikes at one end. The players dig the spikes into the ice to turn left or right.

The sleds for sled hockey have blades underneath, like ice skates.

Sled hockey is a fast game, and players become very fit.
Players speed across the ice,
making turns and hitting the puck
while sitting on their sled.

Keeping Warm and Dry

When playing winter sports, people need to keep warm and dry.

A hat, coat and boots will keep people warm in the snow.

Clothes for winter sports should keep out the wet snow and block the wind.

Staying Safe

While winter sports are lots of fun, they can also be dangerous.

Skiers need to watch out for rocks on snowy slopes.

Many people wear a helmet in case they fall.

Ice skaters need to keep away from thin ice.

It is easy to slip over on ice and snow.

Winter sports can be fast and exciting. During cold months, taking part in winter sports can be a good way to keep fit. It is also a good way to warm up when the weather is icy.

Everyone will have more fun if they play safely.

Glossary

balance (*noun*)	being upright and steady
channel (*noun*)	a ditch, drain or trench
ice rinks (*noun*)	large, flat areas of ice
leap (*verb*)	jump, spring, bound
puck (*noun*)	a flat, rubber disc
runners (*noun*)	long, narrow boards or blades

Index